Disney

ADVENTURES!

Starring your favorite Disney · PIXAR characters!

Illustrated by Art Mawhinney
Additional illustrations by the Disney Storybook Artists

Published by Louis Weber, C.E.O.
Publications International, Ltd.
7373 North Cicero Avenue, Lincolnwood, Illinois 60712

Ground Floor, 59 Gloucester Place, London W1U 8JJ

**Customer Service: 1-800-595-8484 or
customer_service@pilbooks.com**

www.pilbooks.com

p i kids is a trademark of Publications International, Ltd.,
and is registered in the United States.
Look and Find is a trademark of Publications International, Ltd.,
and is registered in the United States and Canada.

8 7 6 5 4 3 2 1

ISBN: 978-1-4127-7146-7

publications international, ltd.

Woody and his friends escape from Sunnyside in a garbage truck that dumps them in a landfill. Ending up here is every toy's greatest fear! Hunt for these broken toys down in the dump with Woody and his friends:

headless doll

action figure

toy truck

stuffed panda

football

toy horse

The Radiator Springs friends arrive in London to help Lightning and Mater! Can you find these cars?

Red

Sally

Sarge

Professor Z

Guido

Ramone

Remy finds himself in the elegant city of Paris, near Gusteau's restaurant. High above the bustling streets, he looks down on all the metropolis has to offer. Look for these food-related shops that might interest Remy:

CAFÉ

CHOCOLATIER

BRASSERIE

CHARCUTERIE

TRAITEUR

PATISSERIE

La Boulangerie

Syndrome's robot is out of control, and Metroville is in danger! It's up to the Incredibles to win this battle and save the town. The grateful public cheers the return of the supers. Can you spot these folks in the crowd?

Mrs. Hogenson

Don Richards

Wendy Day

Firefighter Lopez

Mayor Andrews

Officer O'Leary

Snug Porter

Rusty

John Burrows

It's nighttime in South America. Carl and Russell are resting in the dark with their new friends Kevin and Dug. Keep the four campers company and look for these things that might prove helpful for a night out in the wilderness:

pocketknife

firewood

Wilderness Explorer manual

sleeping bag

compass

tent

Mayhem has broken out in the castle's Great Hall! King Fergus can't believe his eyes when Merida interrupts the fighting. While Merida's bear-mum stays out of sight, scan the crowd for these quarrelsome clansmen:

Nemo has been captured by a human diver! Marlin and his new friend, Dory, swim into dangerous waters to look for clues that will help them find Nemo. Keep an eye out for these scary-looking sharks skulking about in the underwater minefield:

Bruce

Chum

a basking shark

Anchor

a sand shark

a whale shark

a tiger shark

It's chaos at a restaurant in Monstropolis! Boo may be small, but she is causing a lot of trouble. Monsters think human kids are scary! Look for these very important citizens at the scene:

Mayor of Monstropolis

anchorman

Fluffy Poodlepuff

Ellington Kingsley Poodlepuff, IV

Miss Monstropolis

Major Catastrophe

Jean-Pierre LeScare

Dr. Ringworm

Slip back to the landfill to find these metal objects that are ready for recycling:

alarm clock

pot

old lunch box

hammer

can

golf club

Circle back to the London battle and find these Lemon cars defeated by the Radiator Springs crew:

yellow Gremlin

orange Gremlin

purple Hugo

red Hugo

rust-colored Pacer

gray Pacer

Pedal back to Paris and find these bicycles along the busy streets:

❑ red bicycle
❑ blue bicycle
❑ pink bicycle
❑ green bicycle
❑ purplebicycle
❑ yellow bicycle

Go back to the Incredibles' victorious battle in Metroville and sort through the rubble for these pieces of the defeated Omnidroid:

Adventure is out There!

Tiptoe back to Carl and Russell's campsite and find these animals that only come out at night:

Return to the Great Hall to find these things that have been turned into weapons:

Dive down to the submarine with Bruce and his vegetarian friends. Over the years, many divers have visited the sunken sub, but for some reason they can't get out of there fast enough! Can you spot the things they left behind?

- ❑ diver's fin
- ❑ diver's mask
- ❑ underwater flashlight
- ❑ underwater camera
- ❑ weight belt
- ❑ scuba tank

No one is hungry anymore! Go back to the Monstropolis restaurant to find these things no one wants to eat:

- ❑ key slime pie
- ❑ eyeball delight
- ❑ stinky futo maki
- ❑ garbage salad
- ❑ string beans
- ❑ sushi under glass
- ❑ cream of swamp water soup